If Roses Were Blue

Written and illustrated by
Debbie Jenae

Title by
Ashley Kindred

An *Inspired* **101** book

If Roses Were Blue

ISBN #978-0-9889879-1-3
Library of Congress Control Number: 2017901869
Printed in the United States of America.

This is a work of fiction. Names, characters, businesses,
places, events and incidents are either the products of the
author's imagination or used in a fictitious manner. Any
resemblance to actual persons, living or dead, or actual
events is coincidental.

Published by

Inspired 101

P.O. Box 1054, Santa Ynez, CA 93460 USA
Visit us at www.Inspired101.com

10 9 8 7 6 5 4 3 2 1
First Edition

To my daughter Ashley,
for more than words can express
and always in love and light.

Contents

If Roses Were Blue

Chapter 1

Escape

Tell us a story, Chris. Please," begged Theresa, the little girl with long light brown hair.

"Tell you a story?" I repeated, as if I was surprised by the request. They were getting used to my stories.

"Yeah, but not one of those dumb fairy tales. Tell us a different kind of story," Roger suggested. "One we haven't heard before."

I thought for a moment. "I'll tell you what. You wash up at the lake while I catch my breath. When you come back, I'll have a story."

"Last one there is a rotten egg!" shouted Theresa as she jumped up and ran barefoot over the soft grass.

"No fair!" teased Roger as he and Sara chased after her.

I poured myself a tall glass of icy lemonade and took a moment to cool down from the heat of the day and a long round of catch. The air was heavy with a promise of some much-needed rain, but there wasn't a cloud in sight. I stretched out on our blanket, grateful for the shade, and breathed in the beauty of everything around me.

It feels good to be back at Lakeview Park. It has the best beach ever and there is so much to do: golf, tennis, shuffleboard, archery, a children's yard with slides and swings, a huge snack bar, and a heated swimming pool with four diving boards!

Everywhere I look, memories of summers gone by rise up and tickle my senses, including my first dive. It was supposed to be head first without a splash, but it was actually feet first holding my nose.

In my mind, I could still feel the burn as I raced across the soft hot sand pulling at my bare feet until I reached the water's edge. A few steps in and I would flop onto my tire tube, paddle out a bit and float, bobbing up and down among knobby waves.

At some point, my thoughts drifted across the lake to Canada, a whole other country. I couldn't see it from here but, still, I often wondered what life was like on the other side. Just the idea of it seemed to hold so much adventure.

Smiling with the memories, I noticed a seagull glide out over the pool and make a graceful turn toward the wide sandy beach.

There, a single kite flew high in a cloudless sky, unmoving, as if placed on some invisible hook.

Suddenly, it danced a bit, turned and dove straight down with long shiny tails following in pursuit until a new wind scooped it back up and left it to hang once again in the sky.

Beyond and below the kite, the creamy sun-lit sands stretched far along the shore and bubbled with color from umbrellas, beach towels, and people.

Today there is the usual summer breeze skipping across the lake, picking up the smell of suntan lotion, and swirling out past the boardwalk to The Point—my favorite spot in the park. Here, the narrow leaves of giant willow trees glisten in the sunlight and pour into the lake like shimmering green waterfalls. It's a restful place where the hours don't matter and worries get lost in the view.

I wonder why I don't come here more often, especially in the summer. But this summer has been busy with work and getting ready for my last year at college. Still, it is good to get away and wonderful to be here now and spend the day with my younger brother and sister.

I close my eyes as a soft gust flutters over me. From the lake I hear the sounds of endless waves petting the shore mixed with the laughter of Roger, Theresa, and Sara splashing each other.

Roger is eight years old, a scout, and loves to examine things. He says he wants to be a forest ranger or a scientist. Today he brought jars of different sizes and shapes in which to catch creatures "for observation."

Then he would set them free. Roger has a habit of learning a big word and then using it a lot. *Observation* is his latest discovery.

Theresa, Roger's sister, is ten and loves to draw and make things out of just about anything she can find. Last week she gave me a drawing of a willow tree in a frame she covered with sand from the beach.

Sara is Theresa's friend and constant companion since they met three months ago. Unlike Theresa, Sara is often strangely quiet and very shy. She seems happy enough when she's with Theresa, but when adults are around, she draws back into herself, as if she is afraid to move or to speak. Sometimes she is like two different people.

The other night Theresa asked me about something Sara had asked her. It helped me understand a little more. Sara asked Theresa if anyone had ever touched her.

"…You know, down here?" she asked as she glanced down at her lap and quickly looked back up.

Theresa said no and asked why. Instead of answering, Sara drew her attention back to the game they were playing.

"Sara's face turned real red," Theresa said. "I didn't know what to say, Chris. I didn't want to make her feel worse. Should I have asked her what she meant? I think something is wrong."

I told Theresa she could have tried to talk more with her, but Sara may have been too embarrassed or afraid to say anything else. I also told her I was glad she told me.

Since then, I often thought about Sara and wondered just how much she and I might have in common. My concern for her made me realize which story I would tell. Besides, Theresa and Roger know their parents are not my birth parents. It was time to tell them the whole story.

"We're ready, Chris," said Theresa, jarring me from my thoughts.

I settled back against the willow tree. "I'm going to tell you a story about a girl, a little older than you, who had to leave her home because she was afraid."

"You mean she ran away?" asked Sara.

"Well, in a way I guess she did," I said. "And during the days that followed, she learned a lot about trust and courage and love. It changed her life."

Three pairs of eyes stared eagerly up at mine, waiting for me to continue. I closed my own and took a slow, deep breath to draw on some inner strength. I opened my eyes and began.

"Our house was the last house on the right, before the road curved along the top of a tree-covered hill and opened into another group of homes. It was built on the edge of the woods—a small narrow forest that stretched between the river and behind all the houses and neighborhoods leading into the city.

"I used to walk in the woods a lot and hardly ever saw anyone else there. It was like being in another world but just steps away from my own backyard. It was—"

"Is this about you?" interrupted Theresa.

"Yes," I said.

"Is it true?" she asked.

"How old were you?" asked Roger.

"Yes, it's true," I said. "And it was just before my 12th birthday." Pleased by their interest I asked, "May I go on?"

Theresa zipped her mouth closed with a flourish, locked it at the corner, and threw away the invisible key. I continued.

Our house stood on the top of a hill that sloped down into the woods. Most of the hill was covered with trees, but a clearing made a perfect place for winter sledding. Every major snowfall brought kids from around the neighborhood for a contest to see who could go the furthest. One by one, we took that hill as fast and as far as our sleds or saucers could carry us, while dodging anything sticking up through the snow.

The woods in winter was definitely fun, but there was also an emptiness among the bare branches and snow covered paths. It was as if all the color and sweet smells of warmer weather were packed away and protected from the cold.

By summer, towering maple, elm, and oak trees burst with fresh green leaves throwing great shadows over the hills and valleys running through my small forest. Every year they came back like old friends settling in for a nice long visit.

Sometimes I walked down to a special place by the river under a giant oak tree. Big roots that bulged above the ground made a perfect place to sit while I leaned against her trunk. I don't know why, but I always thought of her as feminine, as if it were a grandmother tree with a loving spirit that protected me while I sat in her lap. From there I watched the river barely moving through the wide channel and listened to the woods in quiet conversation. Branches and loose leaves giggled with the wind while birds chirped and chattered about the events in their day.

Anyway, one warm summer afternoon I was swinging in our back yard when my mother appeared in the doorway. She called out a goodbye to my father, who was working in the basement, and walked to the garage.

"Mom," I shouted, pushing myself off the swing and running to her. "Where are you going?"

"I'm going out for a while. I'll be back in a few hours," she said.

"Can I go with you?" I asked hopefully.

"Not this time. You stay here with your father."

My shoulders drooped as I stepped back and watched her car pull out of the driveway, head down around the curve and out of sight.

I didn't want to stay with him. I hated being alone with him. Maybe I should have told her, but what if he finds out? How could she not know? It was all so confusing. I turned slowly toward the house, remembering what happened a few nights before.

———

I had finally fallen asleep when I woke up at the sound of his belt buckle. Except for the light coming from under the closed door, it was totally dark in my room.

"Ssshhh. I just want to make sure you're all tucked in," he whispered. But I knew he didn't come to tuck me in. He wanted to touch me in a way I didn't like.

I didn't say anything. I couldn't move I was so scared. At first I pretended to be asleep, hoping he would just leave me alone. It never worked. His breathing grew louder as he knelt down by my bed. My heart was pounding so hard I thought it would beat right out of my chest.

———

I shook my head to erase the memory and stood staring at the back door. What should I do? Why does it have to be this way? Why can't I tell my mom? I wish Aunt Jennifer hadn't moved. I wish someone would make it stop.

The screeching sound of a power tool shot out from the basement. He was busy with his work. I had to do something!

I crept silently through the dining room, climbed the stairs—being sure to avoid the creaky ones—and entered my bedroom. I grabbed my school bag from the far corner of the closet and quickly checked the contents. An address book, a small package of tissues, and a gift from Aunt Jennifer were still inside. I added my big purple sweater.

After a quick glance around the room, I headed for the door and abruptly froze, startled by a reflection in the mirror. I gasped, thinking someone had caught me, before I realized the reflection was my own yet it was almost like looking at someone else. This girl wore my pink t-shirt and blue shorts, and she had my long blonde hair, but something about her was different— something in her eyes—like nothing was going to stop her. I wasn't sure and couldn't think about it now.

Passing through the kitchen, I grabbed an apple, some cookies, and a juice box. I could still hear the clanging of tools in the basement as I slipped quietly outside.

Behind our house two paths led into the woods. I usually took the one that went straight down the hill. This time I chose the other, starting behind our garage and near the neighbor's fence. Low branches and exposed roots made this path more difficult to follow, at first, but it quickly disappeared among the trees. And, I figured, so would I.

I didn't think about where I would go or when I would come back. I only knew I had to get away, so I kept walking. Leaves and sticks crackled under my feet as I moved deeper into the woods and farther from home.

I followed the winding trail at a steady pace as if it were pulling me along, but I wasn't really paying much attention. Somehow I kept moving until I was so tired I couldn't take another step. As darkness slowly settled in around me, so did a cloud of hopelessness.

Inside a small clearing I sat and leaned against a fallen tree and looked around. I had never gone this far into the woods before. I was frightened and almost wished I had never left.

Where will I go? I have no one now, I thought sadly.

"Hoo, hoo!" cried an owl in the distance.

"Yeah, who?" I answered. Who can I tell? Who would believe me? Who would help me now?

Pushing those thoughts out of my mind, I wrapped my sweater around me, used my bag for support, and shifted into a more comfortable position against the log. I had eaten most of my small supply of food, but I wasn't really hungry. I was just very, very tired. I would be glad when morning came. I was sure I'd know what to do then. After all, things were always better in the morning.

With that glimmer of hope, I curled up in a soft bed of leaves, huddled against the log, and somehow fell into a deep sleep.

Chapter 2

Lady of Light

I woke up during the night feeling as if I were lying on the softest mattress ever made. Tall shadowy pine trees, at first so frightening, now seemed to be standing guard protecting me while I slept. I snuggled under my sweater feeling safe and relaxed.

Still half asleep, I remembered I had been dreaming—a dream I have had many times before. I tried to put myself back into it somehow. It was always the same.

It's a clear summer day. I am standing in a beautiful green meadow lined with full leafy trees. I know I only have to want it badly enough for it to happen. In an instant, I am running as fast as I can down the center of the open field. The grass is a soft cool cushion under my feet and the warm air rushes easily over my skin. Without thinking but with obvious intent, both feet press briefly into the ground as I bend at the knees, extend my arms like wings, and launch myself upward. With little effort I am able to catch rising currents, gradually lifting me higher and higher, until I'm gliding over all the land.

Far below I see people, tiny from this distance, and not able to see me as I circle over the town. But I am drawn to the meadow with grasses and bushy trees in every shade of green against a blue-sky background. I soar above it all freely and at my own wishing. In the morning, I remember my secret flight.

When I opened my eyes again, I thought I was still dreaming. As if a star had come

loose from the sky, a bright light was drifting down through the trees. Unblinking, I watched as it disappeared and reappeared from behind the tree trunks and branches, moving steadily toward the clearing. Now everything around me seemed to be waking up and almost glowing with light and color even though it was still night. Golden brown leaves were nudged and lifted by delicate breezes. Night creatures, too shy to be seen by day, slipped in and out of the shadows.

I had never thought much about fairies or spirits and whether they were real or not. But this place made me wonder.

Then I saw her. She appeared where the light settled, just inside the clearing. That strange, warm white light now seemed to radiate from within her, as if she were the light. Her long straight hair was as black as the night sky still visible through the trees and, like the sky, seemed to hold tiny twinkling stars. She wore a long white sleeveless dress, tapered through the waist that draped in soft folds down to her toes. It, too, sparkled softly hinting of every color with each graceful movement.

For a second she looked directly at me, then turned to the left and nodded ever so slightly toward an owl I had not noticed before, perched on a nearby branch. In that moment, something passed between them—some understanding, but no words were spoken. The owl then lifted and extended its powerful wings and flew off without making a sound.

I stared in awe. She could have stepped straight out of a fairy tale. She also looked quite real, except for the slight glowing, and connected to everything in some way.

Silently, we watched each other. After about a minute she smiled, trusting she had given me enough time to accept what I was seeing. I felt so much warmth and caring from her that I easily smiled back, unafraid, yet curious about who or what she was. Carefully, I sat up not knowing at all what to expect but completely at ease in her presence.

Then she spoke to me, but her mouth didn't move. I honestly think we were reading each other's thoughts! I shook my head and rubbed my eyes, sure I was dreaming now, but nothing changed.

 "Don't be afraid," she said.

"I'm not, really," I said, truthfully.

"You have a question."

"Well…" I hesitated.

"Please, go ahead."

"Well… are you a dream? I mean, if I'm dreaming, can I talk to you even when I know I'm dreaming?"

The tenderness in her eyes reached out to me through her words. "You are not dreaming," she said. "I am as real as you are and I have some wonderful things to tell you."

I pulled my knees close to my chest and leaned in, ready for her to continue.

We talked about many things that night and she always spoke in a calm, gentle manner. She also knew a lot about me, which was strange because I had never seen her before. Still she did seem familiar somehow.

When we talked about my parents, she knew how scared and confused I was by what happened in my house. She understood and said those feelings were very common among people who have been abused.

"But he never hit me," I said suddenly, feeling protective.

"Hitting is just one form of abuse, Chris. He touches your body in ways you don't like. This makes you uneasy. It may not hurt like being slapped across the face, but it hurts you inside. You become afraid and think something must be wrong with you, that somehow what he does is your fault. And he has told you not to tell anyone, hasn't he?"

I nodded.

"He doesn't want anyone to know what he's doing to you because he knows it's wrong. He is the adult and he knows he's not supposed to hurt you. No one, not even a parent, should touch you in ways you don't like. But he does, and you wonder how you can make him stop."

I looked down, feeling a little ashamed for not knowing what to do.

"I know you're afraid to talk to him. Most children being treated in this way are too frightened to say anything or tell anyone else. They keep it a secret and don't get the help they deserve."

I stared at her, surprised to learn there were others.

"Sadly, there are other children who are being hurt in this same way," she said gently.

"I… I guess, I thought it was just me," I stammered. "Everyone else seems so, so normal, like nothing is wrong."

"Children who are mistreated in some way are often threatened or warned not to tell. And it doesn't only happen to girls. Boys are abused, too."

We talked more about my parents. She wanted to know what I thought. When I told her, she didn't make me feel bad or wrong for what I said. Instead, she responded with words or a nod that showed she was truly interested and concerned. She made me feel as if what I thought actually mattered. It felt good to talk about it. It felt good to talk with her.

She knew so many things I had never thought about. She told me everything in the world is alive, not just people and animals.

"Think of all the trees and plants that are growing as living things. In fact, there is movement in all things. You could see this if you could look close enough. Even a rock is made up of tiny particles that move very quickly and too close together for us to see with our eyes alone. Could that also be life?"

I shrugged my shoulders, not knowing what to say.

"I'm telling you this," she explained, "to remind you of something you already know on a much deeper level. Everything has purpose, although it may not always be clear. The light from the moon..." She made a slight upward motion with her hand. "The leaves on the trees and on the ground, the stones in the river. From the largest elephant to the tiniest insect, everything…" She paused, looking directly at me. "Everything has value.

"In a way, we all depend on and influence each other, although we may not be aware of it.

"The rain falling from the sky may put out a forest fire, nourish the plants, feed the rivers that generate food, fill the lake to give you a place to swim, and flow from your faucet into a drinking glass. So the rain becomes a part of everything, even you.

"The reason your woods seemed magical when you awakened was because you were not afraid. You felt a closeness, a connection with the trees, the earth, the air—all things. Instead of being fearful, you were filled with wonder and appreciation. You saw the beauty in the world around you—the beauty that is always there, if we're willing to see.

"You have known much fear and confusion, but don't let that make you afraid of everything. Remember to look with the eyes of your heart, the eyes of your soul. Love the good in everyone. See the beauty in the people you meet. This will help them see the beauty in themselves and those around them.

"Trust in yourself, Chris. You know much more than you realize."

I sat there in a daze. I wanted to remember everything she said because I knew it was important, but there was so much to think about!

She seemed to know this. "Everything we have talked about will become more clear in time and before you see the blue rose."

"Blue rose?" I had never heard of a blue rose. I told her this and her reply was the same.

"But how will I find it?" I asked.

"You won't," she said, "It will find you."

Puzzled by her response, I picked up a small stick and made little circles in the dirt. I loved listening to her and wanted to ask her more.

Feeling a chill, I tossed the stick aside and pulled my sweater a little closer. When I looked up, she was gone.

Chapter 3

Gus

The morning light streamed through the trees and caught a pair of chipmunks at play.

Lying on my side and still a little sleepy, I watched them chase each other through the dried leaves and wished I could join in their game. They played so easily and without a care in the world. Then I realized where I was—far from home and not ready to go back. And what about that fairy lady, the lady of light? She knew all about me. Or had I been dreaming after all?

One of the chipmunks snatched up an acorn, chirped at its partner, and scrambled away. The other darted off as I stood to stretch and brush the leaves off of me.

Maybe I can find a sign that proves she really was here, I thought, as I looked over my forest bedroom. "There must be something," I said aloud and shuffled through the leaves.

"Hey, that's my property you're kickin' around!" shouted a voice from behind me.

Startled, I turned and took a couple steps back. I didn't see anyone.

"Who's there?" I asked a little shaky.

Out from the shadows, atop an old tree stump, appeared a boy about my age and size. He wore blue jeans torn at the knee and almost new tennis shoes. A light green t-shirt hung below his faded jean jacket. A patch of dark brown hair slid across his forehead as he struck a defiant pose, daring me to move or to speak. Yet, somehow he didn't appear quite as tough as he may have wanted me to think.

"Gus is the name. This is my meetin' place, and you're trespassing," he said firmly.

"Well, uh, I'm sorry. I was just tired and I had been walking for a long time and, gosh, I didn't know."

Gus stood a little taller. I think he knew he was making me nervous.

He said, "Well, that's okay, I guess. It's not like you were hurtin' anything. I don't use this place much anymore, anyway. Have you got a name?"

"Chris," I said, thinking what a silly way to ask for someone's name.

Gus jumped off the stump and walked toward me. "So, what are you doing out here anyway?"

"Oh, uh, just going for a walk," I said and quickly added, "to my aunt's house in Woodside."

I certainly wasn't going to tell him why I left and, besides, I knew I would be going there sometime. I liked her a lot. She listened to me and just really seemed to care. Anyway, I didn't plan it at first, but I *was* going in that direction.

"Awful early to be going for a walk," Gus said, narrowing his eyes, as though he didn't really believe me. "And what do you have in that bag?"

Gus reached for my bag with a stick he carried like a sword, but I was quicker. "This is my property," I stated firmly, surprised at my own courage.

"Okay, okay," said Gus. "Just seems like a lot to take on a walk, uh, I mean, to your aunt's house."

"Well, it's not," I said, clutching my bag tightly.

"DROP IT!" yelled Gus moving quickly toward me.

I dropped the bag, alarmed by the sharp tone of his voice, and stepped away. With his stick, he picked up the bag by one strap and tilted it so my things began to fall out. Before I could ask what he thought he was doing with my stuff, out slithered a rather large snake.

"Oh my gosh!" I exclaimed.

"You have to be careful out here. Could be poisonous, but this one's just an ol' garter snake. It won't hurt you," he said.

I stared at the snake as it quickly zig-zagged through the leaves and disappeared. Gus added, "Besides, it's just a little thing."

"A little thing!?" I asked, looking at him as if he were crazy.

"Yeah, it's only about 12 inches from end to end."

A snake's a snake as far as I was concerned.

"In India there are snakes over 12 feet long," Gus stated with authority.

"Lucky I'm not going that far," I mumbled.

I could feel Gus staring at me.

He said, "Looks to me like you could use some help gettin' to your aunt's house."

"Oh, uh, no. That's okay. I'll be fine. I can take care of myself."

As I gathered my things, shaking each one carefully, I glanced toward Gus. He was smiling.

"Leaves," I said in response to his amused look.

"Yeah, sure," said Gus, still smiling. Then, taking this whole matter to heart, he said, "Well, I just happen to be going in that direction and I agree to be your guide."

This time I didn't disagree. Actually, I was a little relieved.

Chapter 4

Prisoner

2 3, 4. Hah! Just try and beat that one," Gus said smugly.

I stepped up to the pond. I placed the smooth, flat stone carefully between my thumb and index finger, resting it at the perfect angle against my middle finger. Slowly and skillfully, I drew my arm back and with a quick flick of my wrist, the stone was released. Flying like a small, round spaceship, it skittered swiftly across the pond.

"…3, 4, 5, 6." Gus counted. "What a lucky pitch!" he teased.

I flashed him that if-you-only-knew kind of look and said, "Not luck. I've had plenty of practice."

Gus turned out to be a pretty good traveling companion. He pointed out plants and trees and told me what he knew about them. Maybe he had been a Boy Scout or something.

We both loved watching animals. It was amazing how easily you could see them if you knew where to look. Gus seemed to know a lot about that. We saw squirrels chasing each other and gathering food. Gus pointed out rabbit holes and gopher holes, although I'm still not sure which is which.

Later we saw something rustling through the leaves along a dry creek bed and thought it might be a raccoon. Of course, it was gone by the time we reached the spot where we saw the movement. That led to some more wandering that brought us to the pond.

I wasn't sure where we were exactly. Gus had said we were heading north, so I guess we were heading north. Besides, it didn't really matter; I was having so much fun.

Gus stood ready to skip another stone across the pond but stopped and lifted his nose to the air. "Do you smell that?" he asked.

"It smells like a barbecue," I said.

"Come on," said Gus. "I think it's coming from over there."

Gus crept through the trees like a secret agent. He could be so dramatic. I ended up doing the same thing as we moved carefully and quietly, following our noses toward that wonderful smell. We had already shared my apple, which was all the food I had left. I wondered why Gus didn't bring anything to eat and hoped he couldn't hear my stomach growling.

As we followed the narrow path around a hill, the smell grew stronger. It was definitely food. My mouth watered as tasty pictures flashed through my mind.

We stopped behind some bushes and watched a faint column of smoke rise from a clearing not far ahead. I crouched on one knee, as Gus was doing, and kept very still as we peered through the bushes.

Gus pulled a small telescope out of his pocket and scanned the area like a captain at sea on the lookout for whales or far off islands. I smiled. Any minute he would cry out, "Land ho!" or "Thar she blows!"

Gus signaled for me to come closer, handing me the telescope. I held it to my eye and aimed it in the direction he was pointing.

Through the trees I saw a small campfire burning inside a circle of rocks. Leaning against the rocks were sticks with something stuck on the end. Hot dogs!

Letting my stomach take control, I gave the telescope back to Gus and started to get up. He grabbed my arm and pulled me back down pointing to the left and away from the campfire. Two older teenagers stood talking to each other. The boy shook his head, as if in disagreement, and reached into the end of a log and pulled out a bag he carried to the fire. Carefully, he took things out of the bag and put them on the ground.

"What are they doing?" I whispered.

45

Gus turned to me and in a low, quiet voice said, "They have jewelry and some other stuff. I'll bet they stole it."

"What are we going to do?" I asked, looking at Gus. Suddenly I wasn't so hungry and the possibility of being discovered by criminals was way too creepy. I tugged at Gus's jacket and said, "Let's get out of here."

Without saying a word, Gus tapped my arm and motioned again toward the clearing. The girl was walking back to the fire with something in her arms. It was a small dog!

Gus backed up, intent on getting a better view. I still didn't like the looks of this, but I was now just as curious to find out what was going on. I followed right on his heels to a large tree covered mound. Lying low we could hear what they were saying without being seen.

"I don't know why you had to bring that stupid dog, Holly. It's just going to slow us down," said the boy looking over each item he'd removed from the bag. He sounded angry.

"It's not a stupid dog, Mace, and besides I kind of like him. He seems real smart and I'll bet he's a purebred of some kind. Did you see this collar? It's real pretty. I think—"

"What did you say?" interrupted Mace, walking toward the dog.

"The collar. It's pretty," she said, stroking the dog's hair.

"No, no, before that. Something about bread?" Mace reached out to the dog who promptly growled and snapped at him.

Holly laughed and tried to explain. "Not bread like for a sandwich. Purebred. B-r-e-d," she spelled. "That means it's not a mix of different kinds of dogs. I think it's

47

a Yorkshire Terrier. That pet shop where I worked had one just like it."

Mace tried again. "That's a good boy." The dog snapped a second time.

"Ain't they worth a lot of money?" asked Mace.

"Oh, yeah. We had one at the store that sold for $1,000."

Mace again reached out to the dog, tempting him with a piece of meat. The dog growled.

"Well, maybe we better take care of this mutt for a while. I've got me a real good idea—OW! It bit me!" he yelped.

"What do you expect? You were so mean to him back at the house." Holly said with obvious disapproval.

"He wouldn't shut up! We coulda got caught, ya know," said Mace inspecting his wound. Then he added, "Well, you can take care of it. I got plans."

"What do you mean?"

"I think they would pay quite a bit to get their precious *pure* bred back," he said mockingly.

Mace sat down and again studied the items he had taken from the bag.

"I want to keep it," stated Holly. "I always wanted a dog of my own. Besides, we can get some money when we sell that jewelry."

"Forget it," commanded Mace. "We'll need that money, too, and we might get a lot for that dog. Then we can get far away from this place."

Gus and I had heard enough. Without a word, we retraced our steps until we were a safe distance away from their camp.

One thing I learned about Gus was he had a deep respect for animals. He was worried about the dog. I was, too. And I knew, even before I asked, that he had a plan.

"Well?" I asked, turning to Gus.

He met my gaze and for a moment searched my face. With a raised eyebrow, a tilt of his head, and absolute conviction, he said, "I have to save the dog."

I could see it in his eyes; he wanted my help.

Chapter 5

Rescue

We talked about rescue plans while we waited to see what Holly and Mace would do. Finally, Mace put out the fire and Holly tied the dog to a tree. They left, taking the bag with them.

We decided to wait a few minutes to make sure they were well on their way. I nervously peeled the bark off of sticks I found around me, while Gus used his telescope to survey the area. Finally, Gus turned toward me and whispered, "Let's go." We didn't know how long they would be gone, so we had to work fast.

We headed into their camp from different directions. If Holly and Mace came back too soon and one of us was caught, the other one could go for help. I moved around to the left, and Gus went to the right. We both listened for sounds of their return.

Although we tried to creep along as quietly and quickly as possible, the dog heard us and broke the silence with non-stop barking. Gus reached him first. The dog stopped barking, wagged his tail, and jumped all over Gus, licking him in appreciation. You'd have thought they were old friends.

Gus spoke soothingly, "It's okay, boy. You're safe now."

"Come on, Gus," I whispered, looking over my shoulder. "We need to get out of here."

Gus carried the dog as we ran back the way we came. Stopping for a minute to catch our breath, Gus said, "Oh, rats! I forgot the hot dogs."

He pushed the dog at me. "Here, hold him. I'll be right back. Meet me at the pond."

I started to tell him to forget the food, but he was already out of sight.

I walked back to the pond. As I waited, I took a closer look at the animal we had just rescued sitting patiently in my lap.

I have never seen this kind of dog before. Holly called it a Yorkshire Terrier. He had a cute face, with huge brown eyes and a narrow nose that reminded me of a fox. But unlike a fox, this dog's hair was long and fine and in some places stuck out in different directions. His ears pointed straight up and twisted from front to back as he listened to all the sounds around us. He sure was cute, and I gave him a hug. He gave me a quick, licky kind of kiss and went back to watching for Gus.

Soon I began to worry. What if Mace and Holly came back? Was Gus okay? I listened hard, but heard only the chattering of birds and the breeze rustling the leaves.

Finally, I caught sight of him moving swiftly in my direction.

"Did you get the hot dogs?" I asked.

He took a moment to catch his breath and pet the dog. "I didn't see any," he said, disappointed. "They must have eaten them all. But…" and he unzipped his jacket, "they left these."

Grinning, he produced a bag of tortilla chips and one root beer from his jacket.

The two of us sat by the pond sharing what little food we had. The dog liked chips, too, and kept inching closer to Gus waiting for another treat.

Watching them, I wondered about Gus. He easily showed concern for this dog and other animals we came across. But when I asked about him, his answers were short or he changed the subject. Maybe he didn't want me to know too much about him. It didn't really matter now because I knew how caring he could be and that made me smile.

Without looking up, Gus muttered, "Thanks."

"For what?" I asked, taking another drink.

"For helping me rescue the dog. Most people wouldn't care, but you did, and it was real brave of you to help."

Brave. Me? Funny he should say that. I don't think I'm brave at all. It seems like I'm always scared and worried something bad is going to happen.

I leaned back on my elbows and gazed up at the treetops swishing softly against a pale blue sky. Something the lady said last night was beginning to make more sense. She was talking about seeing the good in people and how what we do can affect others without our knowing it.

"Remember when you used to sit on the dock and drop pebbles into the water and watch rings form in circles around the center?"

Now how did she know that, I wondered?

She smiled and continued, "And more rings formed and moved out from the center? A simple sincere smile can have the same effect—touching the hearts of others and encouraging them to share a kindness, like a smile, creating ripples of love that move out into the world.

"Too much fear and unkind actions can have a similar reach but in a negative way. Don't be afraid of your feelings, Chris, or to show you care. Let fear remind you to be safe without letting it take over. You are stronger than you think. See the beauty within and around you and watch it grow."

It wasn't clear to me then. How could I see things that weren't there? And I sure didn't feel very strong sometimes, but her words gave me hope. She said to think of it as a place of strength in everyone, a loving place. The more we accept and connect with that space in ourselves, the more we understand.

Gosh, it's almost like she's still here!

I looked at Gus. He was gently petting the dog that had now curled up in his lap.

"You're the brave one," I said, "Besides I should thank you."

"For what?" he said, looking up.

"For being my friend," I said quietly.

Tossing stones into the water, I stole a sideways glance at Gus. He was smiling. Maybe he had found a friend, too.

Chapter 6

The Ceremony

We finished our chips and root beer lunch and, still heading toward Woodside, explored along a stream. Gus tied the dog to a bush so he could show me some reeds. He split one of the reeds open and pointed to the spongy stuff inside that he called Indian gum.

"Here, try some." He pulled out a strip, tore it in half, and handed a piece to me.

I hesitated. It looked like a piece of cotton jump rope. I squeezed it flat between my fingers and dropped it in the palm of my hand. Slowly it filled back out to its original shape, kind of like a dry sponge.

"Go ahead, it's not poison," he said as he popped a piece into his mouth.

Okay, I thought, and carefully chewed a small piece. "It tastes like cardboard."

"Yeah," laughed Gus. "Pretty chewy though, huh?" Then he asked, "When did you eat cardboard?"

Cute, I thought, and made a face at him. As we turned and spit out our *gum*, we heard growling. The dog had pulled the rope free and was hopping in and out of the bushes at the edge of a small pond.

A squirrel shot out from the bushes, jumped across the pond, and scampered up a tree.

The dog also shot out of the bushes, but instead of jumping over, he slipped and landed in the pond. Covered with mud and green slime, he ran to the base of the tree and barked excitedly at the squirrel now well out of reach. After a quick body shake, he turned toward us, saw the loose end of the rope, picked it up in his teeth, and trotted over to Gus.

"Oh, yuck!" said Gus, holding the rope away to keep the dog from touching him. "You smell awful!"

I laughed as I watched Gus trying so hard to keep his muddy, smelly friend from getting too close. The harder he tried to push the dog away, the more the dog lunged at him playfully.

"We're going to have to give him a bath," I said, reaching for my bag.

"Too bad we don't have any soap," Gus replied.

"I do," I said, shuffling through my bag.

"You brought soap?!"

"It was a gift from my aunt. She went to Hawaii. Here it is."

I unrolled a long, thin rectangle of fabric printed with bright tropical flowers, called a *pareu* (pronounced "pa-ray-oo"). Three small containers—a bottle of shampoo, a tube of hand lotion, and a tin of body powder—appeared within the folds. I handed him the shampoo and off we went.

When we arrived at the stream, we took off our socks and shoes and Gus rolled up his pant legs. I helped him remove the collar and re-tie the rope around the dog's neck so he couldn't run off. After putting the collar in my pocket, I held the rope while Gus quickly rinsed and soaped and rinsed the dog.

Following the bath, I handed the pareu to Gus to use as a towel while I found a spot in the shade to sit and examine the collar. It was pretty, as Holly said, but it needed polishing. I pulled a tissue from my bag and began cleaning. As I wiped away the dirt, the colored stones sewn into the top sparkled against the light blue leather band. I turned it over to work on the inside. To my surprise an address and phone number appeared under the dirt I wiped away.

"Gus!" I called. "His name is Cody."

"Hey!" shouted Gus, as he wrestled his shoe away from the dog.

"Look at this," I said, walking over to him. "This must be where he lives."

Gus finished tying his shoe and looked at the inside of the collar.

"Yeah, well, that saves us a lot of time finding out who he belongs to," he said sharply.

"But this could also be the house they robbed," I said, surprised at his anger.

"Yeah, one of 'em," said Gus, his tone still sharp.

"What do you mean? Do you know where this is?" I asked.

"Yeah, I oughta. I used to live there."

"In this house?"

"No, a couple blocks from there."

I thought for a moment, considering his short answers and the quick change in his mood.

"Did you run away?" I asked.

"Takes one to know one," said Gus, watching the dog shake from his bath.

"Why did *you* leave?" I asked carefully.

Cody ran over and sat next to Gus. I handed him the collar and he gently put it around the dog's neck. Now I see why Gus seemed angry. He really liked this dog and probably hoped he could keep him.

"Cody . . . It fits him," he said to no one in particular.

Then to answer my question, he said, "I just didn't like it there, that's all."

"Yeah, I know what you mean," I said thoughtfully. Part of me wanted to tell Gus why I left and part of me didn't. I had never told anyone.

I was trembling. Gus must have noticed because he seemed truly concerned when he asked, "Why, what happened to you?"

"I asked you first," I said, still not sure if I should tell.

"It's no big deal," said Gus. "Both my parents work so they're not home much. Even when they are, they don't know I'm there. They're too busy with their jobs and their friends. Sometimes, I think they don't want me around anymore. Anyway, they went away for a couple of days, so here I am."

"You did run away!" I declared.

"Not exactly," said Gus. "My dad keeps promising to take me camping and never does, so I decided I would camp out by myself for a few days."

"By yourself?"

"Sure, why not?"

I didn't answer remembering how I had set out alone just the day before.

"Do your parents know? I mean, did you ever tell them how you feel?"

"I tried to but they're always too busy. You know how sometimes people nod like they hear you, but you know they're not really listening? 'Run along and play,'" he said, mimicking them.

I felt sad for Gus. He said it was no big deal, but I could tell it bothered him a lot. He just hides how he feels because he thinks no one will listen, no one will care. I do the same thing.

After a moment I asked, "Did you bring anything to eat?"

"Yeah, sort of," he said, still a little lost in his thoughts.

"What do you mean, 'sort of'?"

"Well, I was supposed to go to a friend's house until my brother got off work. As usual, my parents left in such a hurry they didn't have time to drop me off. So I decided I wouldn't go to my friend's house or stay with my brother. I'd go camping instead. I just started to pack some food when I heard someone in the driveway. I didn't even grab my stuff. I just took off."

I nodded and said, "I guess we both left in a hurry."

Gus looked at me curiously. "What about you?" he said as he softly petted the dog who had stretched out next to him.

My heart hammered against my chest, as if my long kept secret was going to burst out on its own. I knew I was going to tell him. I was going to trust him just as he had trusted me. I wondered what he would think but I began anyway.

"Sometimes my father comes to my room at night or he finds me when we're alone in the house. Sometimes he touches me… all over… in ways I don't like. I just hate it." I had to stop for a moment. My throat tightened making my voice crack. I swallowed hard and took a deep breath.

I couldn't look at Gus; I was so embarrassed. But I couldn't lie anymore or pretend everything was okay.

"Yesterday my mom had to go out. I wanted to go with her, but she said I had to stay home with my dad. I just got scared and knew I couldn't stay there. So I left."

Gus listened silently.

A quick look passed between us. He knew what I was feeling.

"Does anyone else know?" he asked.

"No. He always told me not to tell. So I never did… until now."

"Does your mom know?"

"I don't think so. I don't know. I wanted to tell her, but I was too scared. And if I did tell her, what would she do? I'm not sure she would believe me. And what if he found out that I told? I just want it to stop." Tears were stinging at my eyes. "I try so hard to be good, so they will love me and not hurt me, but I guess I'm always doing something wrong."

"Hey," insisted Gus. "You didn't do anything wrong. It's not your fault. You seem pretty great to me. Anyone who doesn't like you is just plain crazy. Besides, we have to believe in ourselves. Who else have we got?"

I stared at Gus, not believing my ears. He was saying the same thing the lady said last night! At that thought, a warm, safe feeling flowed through me as I remembered our conversation in the clearing. Maybe this was the energy she talked about.

She had also said it was not my fault and that my father is confused and afraid.

"Is he afraid of me?" I asked. I thought adults weren't supposed to be scared.

"Not really," she answered. "He's afraid someone will find out what he's doing to you, and he can't seem to stop.

"It's not your fault, Chris, and it's not because of something you have done. There isn't anything you can say or do that gives someone a right to hurt you.

"Your parents need help and your father has to understand that what he is doing to you is wrong.

"This may be difficult for you to believe, but too often your father feels helpless, as if anything he might say or do doesn't matter. He hides this by making others afraid of him. This is part of the reason why he touches you in ways that he shouldn't. It makes him feel in control of something and more powerful—for a while.

"Your mother knows something is wrong, but she has chosen to ignore it. She may not want to believe it and may have many reasons to be afraid, which make her unable to protect you. They are both caught up in the troubles of their lives, problems that have nothing to do with you.

"It's all very complicated, but it's important to understand that, although you are the one being hurt, it is not really about you or because of you. It is only directed at you because you happen to be there. This does not change your value as a person. You are lovable and acceptable exactly as you are.

"They need help to see that they can learn and change in ways that are best for everyone. Do you understand?"

By confiding in Gus just now, I understood more of what she said last night. I hoped that nothing like this had ever happened to Gus, but I also knew he understood. He doesn't feel wanted and I don't feel wanted the way I would like. We have the same feelings but not from the same experiences. She was right. It is complicated.

"You know what?" asked Gus, his words shaking me from my thoughts. "We're a lot alike, you and me. We could be a blood brother and sister, you know, like the Native Americans used to do."

"We don't have to draw blood, do we?" I asked remembering a story I'd read.

"Heck, no," said Gus, "But we could give each other something. That way we would always remember this time and what we did and what we talked about. We could make a pact."

As I watched Gus pick up and discard a number of sticks, I realized how much better I felt. I'm glad I told him. He believed me. He didn't fix anything for me—he didn't have to—but he cared enough to listen to every word. I would not forget that.

We decided to seal our pact with a ceremony. We sat on the ground, facing each other. With his carefully chosen stick, he drew a circle in the dirt between us and gently placed the stick in the center cutting the circle in half. Slowly he removed a ring from his finger. It was a very unusual ring made of silver metal circles linked together like a chain.

He held the ring tightly in his fist, raised his hand to the sky, and proclaimed, "Let all witness—"

It was so dramatic but I loved it! Beaming with a mixture of pride and affection, I lowered my head to look down at the circle as Gus continued.

"—my special promise to Chris. From this day forward, no matter what happens, I am her friend. I will always listen if she needs someone to talk to, and I will always help in any way I can. This ring is my symbol of our eternal friendship." He placed the ring in the center of the half-circle in front of me.

The air swirled around us as if to capture his promise for all time. It was a moment I will never forget because I knew he meant every word he said.

From my wrist I removed the friendship bracelet I had made with different colored stretchy string. Holding the bracelet in my lap I said, "I will always remember this day. Even though we really just met, it's like we've been friends forever. I promise that if you ever need anything or just want to talk, I will always be there for you, too. This is my symbol of our eternal friendship." I placed the bracelet in the center of his half circle.

"By the way," said Gus, "my name is Mark."

"Mark? Why did you tell me it was Gus?" I asked surprised.

"Oh, I don't know. I didn't know who you were, and it sounded kinda tough, I guess. Anyway, everybody calls me Gus." He paused, retying the laces on his shoe and then added, "I just wanted you to know."

"You don't need a tough sounding name," I said. "Which one do you like better?"

"I like 'Gus'," said Mark.

"Then that's what I'll call you," I declared.

Silently, Gus slipped my bracelet on his left wrist while I tried his ring on a couple of fingers before finding the best fit on my right hand.

"Hand me the stick," he whispered, as if to remind me of my unspoken duty.

I picked up the stick, respectful of its honorable purpose in the ceremony, and handed it to him.

He held the stick in both hands and raised it high over his head. "To seal our pact!" he announced, and brought the stick crashing down, breaking it over his knee.

Chapter 7

Hostage

Cody loved to explore and was always sniffing and digging for some hidden doggie treasure. This time he pulled loose as Gus was removing bits of leaves and sticks that were stuck in the dog's hair. We finally caught up with him as he nosed around an old hollow tree. While Gus and Cody poked in the tree, I went back to a patch of violets we passed during the chase.

The afternoon sun streamed through openings in the trees warming the day as I strolled along the narrow path. The small purple flowers were easy to spot out in the open where they absorbed the light making their color so much brighter.

Suddenly, my entire body stiffened. Every cell was on high alert, straining to hear what might have caused the alarm. I tilted my head to tune in even more. Nothing, but I had immediately thought of Gus.

I ran as quietly as I could back along the path toward the hollow tree until I heard unpleasant yet familiar voices. Slowing my pace I hid behind some large rocks and was just able to make out what they were saying.

"Where'd you get the dog?" someone shouted angrily.

My fear was confirmed when I heard Gus speak next.

"I told you I found him tied to a tree and figured someone just left him there."

"Stealing the dog, eh?" came Mace's accusing reply.

"There was no one around and it didn't look like anyone was coming back. I wasn't stealing him."

Cody was barking wildly. He probably thought Mace would hurt Gus.

"Yeah, sure. Holly, keep that thing quiet!" snarled Mace.

I slowly peeked around the rock. Holly was holding the rope tied to Cody. Gus was sitting on the ground with Mace standing over him. I wondered why Gus didn't say more. Then I realized he didn't want them to know what we knew. They were the actual thieves. Gus also hadn't mentioned me.

"What are you doing out here anyway?" asked Mace, almost spitting out the words.

"I thought I knew a short cut through the woods, but I guess I got lost," Gus explained, trying to sound convincing.

"Well, the path is over that way. Why don't you go find it," Mace commanded impatiently.

"Yeah, sure," agreed Gus.

"Come on, Holly," ordered Mace. After a few steps, he spun around and glared at Gus, "By the way, kid, I won't say anything about you takin' our dog." He confirmed the threat with narrowed eyes and a tight jaw.

"Thanks, mister," said Gus. "Nice dog you've got there."

Cody squirmed in Holly's arms as they trudged off.

As soon as Holly and Mace were out of sight, I ran over to Gus.

"Gus, are you okay?"

"Yeah, yeah. I hurt my ankle, though. We tried to hide when I heard them coming, but I tripped. Ohhh," he groaned as he tried to stand and sat back down.

"What can I do?" I asked.

"Well, we have to get Cody back." started Gus.

"I know that, I mean about your ankle?"

"Oh, it'll be okay. I just can't walk on it very well right now."

"I can help you," I said with determination and turned away from him.

"You call that helping, leaving me layin' here like this?" Gus whined.

I glanced back. Gus flashed me a wide fake smile.

Oh, geez, I thought to myself.

"Just kidding," said Gus, obviously happy with his performance. "What are you lookin' for?"

"Something to help you walk. I thought we could make a crutch," I said as I tested some thick branches.

"Good idea!" he said, approvingly.

I blushed a little at the compliment and turned away so he wouldn't notice. Then I spotted the perfect branch for a crutch, and decided my sweater would make a soft cushion.

As I was tying the sleeves around the branch, Gus asked, "Do you really have an Aunt Jennifer?"

"Yes," I said. "Well, sort of. She's not really my aunt. I've just always called her that. She and my mom were best friends when she lived closer to us. I used to see her a lot. She liked to cook and would invite me over to her house to help, especially when she made cookies. Since she moved to Woodside, I haven't seen her much, even though it isn't all that far."

"Is that where you're going?" asked Gus.

"I guess so."

"Are you going to tell her?"

"Yeah, I think so. I'm scared though, Gus. Do you think I should?"

"If you think she'll believe you, then you should tell her. You have to tell someone who can help."

"I think she'll help me," I said. At least I was pretty sure she would.

Getting out of the woods was a slow and painful process at first. Gus had trouble using the crutch, but it became easier as we went along.

The painful part came when we were walking up a steep hill leading to the road. I was helping Gus when he pointed at a hawk, circling overhead. With our next step, the crutch went into a hole and down we went, landing in a tangled heap. I suppose we could have been hurt, but actually it was pretty funny— looking up and then falling down.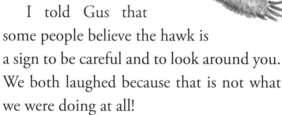

I told Gus that some people believe the hawk is a sign to be careful and to look around you. We both laughed because that is not what we were doing at all!

When we reached the road, Gus mentioned that his ankle felt better. Besides, a little thing like a sore ankle wasn't going to slow Gus down. At least, that's what he said.

"Hey, I know where we are," Gus said as he looked around. "There's a store at the end of the next block. They should have a phone."

Neither one of us said much as we walked toward the store. But I thought about Gus and how much fun we had and wondered if I would ever see him again. It was hard to believe that so much had happened in only two days.

Just before entering the store, Gus asked if we should call our parents. I told him I wasn't ready to talk to them yet. He nodded. "Me neither. Let's find Cody first."

We briefly explained our situation to the man behind the counter and asked if we could use his phone. He pulled a phone from under the counter and handed it to me. I called Aunt Jennifer. It rang and rang. I turned to Gus.

"We'll call Jack," he said, seeing my look of disappointment.

The man offered Gus a phone book. Gus thanked him and flipped through the pages.

I asked, "Who's Jack?"

"My brother," said Gus, like I should know.

"Oh, the one you were supposed to stay with?"

"Yeah. Here it is. Delightful Deli. It's a sandwich place. He works there."

Gus contacted his brother at the deli. After a quick explanation, Jack agreed to meet us at a nearby park.

On the way, I hoped Jack wouldn't be mad at Gus or, worse yet, be mad at me and call my parents—or call the police! But when we all met at the park, I could see he was as nice as Gus and wanted to help. He even brought a submarine sandwich cut in pieces for us to share. It was the best sandwich ever!

Jack and Gus agreed that Cody probably belonged to the Bensons who lived at the address printed on the collar. Jack used to deliver newspapers and the Benson house was on his route.

Gus wanted Jack to understand. "We have to help Cody, Jack. They don't care about him. They just want the money."

"Okay, okay," said Jack. "But what about Mom and Dad? I had to call them when I couldn't find you. They're really worried about you, you know? They're even coming back early. We have to let them know you're all right."

"You didn't tell them, did you Jack?" implored Gus.

"No, I haven't talked to them since you called me, but we need to call them."

"Okay," said Gus, "but I want to get Cody back first."

"No," insisted Jack as he pulled out his cell phone. "First we call Mom and Dad."

Jack left a message that Gus was safe, then picked up his sandwich and turned his attention to me.

"And what about you? You ran away, too, eh? I'm sure your folks are worried."

"I don't think so," I said. "Besides, I'm going to my Aunt Jennifer's house. I'll call her after we find Cody."

"Boy, you two are pretty thick. All right. I'll help, but then I'm taking you both home. Deal?"

"Deal," said Gus and I, and the three of us shook hands.

Chapter 8

New Friends

After we finished eating, Jack called the deli to make sure the afternoon shift was covered. Then we drove to the address printed on the inside of Cody's collar.

The Bensons lived in a two-story, brick house with white trim around the windows. A round white column stood on each side of the covered front porch. In front of each column at the base of the steps, a large pot overflowed with red, white, and deep purple flowers.

We followed Jack to the front door where he rang the doorbell. We waited. He tried again.

I wondered what we would do if no one was home. Just then the door opened. A man, very formally dressed, stood there holding a dishtowel. He looked us over, raised an eyebrow, and with no expression asked, "Can I help you?"

"We would like to speak to Mr. and Mrs. Benson," stated Jack.

"They are not at home at the moment," replied the man, rather stiffly.

"It's awful important," insisted Gus. "It's about Cody."

"Cody?" repeated the man.

"Cody. Their dog," I said.

"Yes, of course, their dog. Do you have this dog?"

"No," said Gus, "but we know who does, and we want to talk to the Bensons about getting him back."

"I see. Mr. and Mrs. Benson will be back soon. I'm quite sure they would wish to speak to you. Perhaps you would care to come in and wait?"

"Thank you. We will," said Jack.

Inside was the most beautiful home I had ever seen. A white tiled hallway stretched to the back of the house. Creamy tan walls were lined with bright paintings. An open staircase climbed in a curve to the second floor.

As we followed the man down the hall, I glanced quickly through the first open door. Shelves filled with books covered the whole far wall surrounding a picture window with a garden view. To the left of the window, a shiny black piano faced an overstuffed blue and white couch as if expecting an audience.

In another room a long table with twelve chairs caught my eye. They must have a lot of company! I could just imagine the people who lived here strolling down the stairway, led by the guy who answered the door, and into the dining room to greet their dinner guests.

The hallway ended near the kitchen at a set of double doors overlooking the patio and the backyard. Once outside, we sat in heavy white iron chairs with fluffy cushions at a glass-topped table. The butler—or whatever he was—brought us some ice water and returned to the kitchen.

Soon we heard voices coming from inside the house.

A very elegant couple passed through the doors the butler held open. The man had dark hair speckled with silver and was dressed in dark blue jeans and a reddish brown v-neck sweater. The woman wore her curly light brown hair loosely pinned up. Her slacks were also light brown topped with a white shirt and a long chocolate colored jacket. She smiled warmly at us and handed her briefcase to the butler as she came outside.

"Well, hello there," said the man with a friendly smile. "Thank you, Taylor," he said to the butler to excuse him. He waited a moment for Taylor to go back in the house before continuing.

"That's our house manager. He takes care of things around here." Then he leaned forward and whispered, "A little stuffy, but a good man."

That brought smiles all around and helped us to relax.

"Well now," announced the man as he leaned against the brick barbecue, "I'm Michael Benson and this is my wife Nancy.

We understand you might know about Cody."

Gus told them how he and I found Cody with the two dog-nappers. He also told them about the jewelry. When we explained how we rescued Cody, both the Bensons looked impressed. They listened, nodded, and never interrupted. They were so nice!

When we finished with the details, Mr. Benson twirled his wedding ring thoughtfully. I was getting nervous; no one was saying anything.

Mr. Benson looked at Jack. "You look familiar, young man. Have we met before?"

Jack said, "I used to deliver your newspaper, sir."

"That's right," said Mr. Benson, remembering. "Best paper boy we ever had. Always square on the front porch. Helped you fix your bike once, if I recall."

"You sure did," said Jack, smiling. "The chain kept coming off. You helped me fix it one morning before you left for work."

"How's your bike now?"

"Belongs to Gus," said Jack, nodding in Gus's direction. "I'm the assistant manager at the deli in town," he added, proudly.

Gus and I exchanged glances. What was all this bike talk about? We both turned to the Bensons and said, "We can get Cody back."

"Do you know if they still have Cody?" asked Mrs. Benson.

"They may have tried to contact you," said Jack.

"Taylor?" called Mr. Benson, turning toward the house.

Taylor appeared instantly. "Yes, sir?"

"Always close at hand, aren't you, Taylor?"

"I try to be, sir."

"Well done. Bring me the mail and any messages, would you please?"

"Certainly." Taylor turned and walked back into the house.

Mr. Benson said that he and his wife had been out most of the day. Maybe someone had tried to call.

Taylor returned with the mail and telephone messages. In the stack was a folded sheet of paper marked:

YOUR DOG

Inside was a handwritten note:

FOUND YOUR DOG.
$500 WOULD BE A GOOD REWARD
BRING TO THE BRYANT PARK FOUNTAIN
THIS SUNDAY 9:00 PM. COME ALONE.

After reading the note to us, Mr. and Mrs. Benson decided to call the police. The robbery had already been reported, but the police should know about the note.

Gus and I were disappointed. We wanted to rescue Cody again.

Gus said, "We can help. We know what they look like."

"You seem awfully concerned about our dog, young man," said Mr. Benson, smiling at Gus.

"Well, I know they don't want Cody, they just want the money."

I knew there was more behind Gus's remark. He loved Cody and would go after those two by himself if he had the chance!

The police said we could expect Detective Sheaffer to arrive in an unmarked car within the hour. There was a chance the thieves were watching the house. Mr.

Benson suggested we call our parents to let them know where we were.

I froze at the mention of my parents. Too many thoughts and pictures raced through my mind. I couldn't go back now. I wasn't ready. Besides, I was sure they would be really mad at me for leaving. I just couldn't let them call. Not yet.

Meanwhile, Gus threw a troubled look at Jack that didn't go unnoticed.

"You have all been very helpful to us," said Mr. Benson, "but we have to let the police do their job. They're trained for this type of work."

"He's right," agreed Jack.

"But you don't know what they look like," pleaded Gus, looking from Jack to Mr. Benson.

"That's what you'll tell the detective. It's safer for you both this way," assured Mr. Benson.

"Are you all right, dear?" asked Mrs. Benson, placing her hand over mine.

I couldn't say anything. I didn't know what to say. Everything in the last two days—the lady in the woods, meeting Gus and the fun we had, and just feeling better about myself—was getting mixed in with everything else. I couldn't sort it out. I lowered my head to hide the truth in my face.

Quickly Gus said, "Her parents are out of town. You'll have to call her Aunt Jennifer. Right, Chris?"

Saved! I could have hugged him right then and there!

"That's right," I managed to say.

Mr. and Mrs. Benson looked at each other for a moment and then back at me.

"What is your Aunt Jennifer's last name?" asked Mrs. Benson.

"Walters," I said.

"Let's go call her," she suggested as she stood up.

I hesitated. What would I say to her? She didn't even know I was coming.

I followed Mrs. Benson into the kitchen where she handed me the phone. I entered the number. It rang several times with no answer.

"There's no one home now," I said as I handed her the phone.

Mrs. Benson led me to the window seat. "Is there something else, Chris? You seem upset."

I shook my head and looked down at my hands. I just couldn't tell her I was afraid to go home.

Mrs. Benson said gently, "I'm a very good listener. Sometimes it helps just to talk about things. What is scaring you, dear? Are you afraid to go home?"

I nervously twisted Gus's chain ring around my finger, painfully aware of the concerned and patient gaze of Nancy Benson. I would always remember our ceremony and the look in Gus's eyes when I told him. He believed me, but would she? I couldn't go back home. Not now, not yet. I had to trust her.

I nodded and when I did, Mrs. Benson took my hand and held it in both of hers. "What's going on?" she asked.

I told her what happened at home, about my dad, and why I was going to Aunt Jennifer's. And I told her how I met Gus.

"He's wonderful," I said. "Best friend anyone could ever have."

"I can see that," said Mrs. Benson. "You two have a very special friendship. It sounds to me like your parents need some help, though. But right now I want to help you, Chris. Is that okay with you?"

I nodded again.

She said, "You're very brave, Chris. Thank you for trusting me enough to tell me."

She hugged me then—a safe, comforting hug.

We joined the others on the patio just as the detective arrived. He took lots of notes as we told our story. Thanking us for the information, he flipped the cover of his notebook closed and said he would do all he could to get Cody back. Mr. and Mrs. Benson walked the detective to his car.

When the Bensons returned, they insisted we stay for dinner. "That's another thing about Taylor," confided Mr. Benson. "He's an exceptional cook."

"But, sir, you gave me the evening off—the concert, in town?" reminded Taylor when hearing of the dinner plans.

"Oh, blast it, that's right. You go ahead, Taylor. We'll manage just fine." Turning to us, Mr. Benson suggested, "How about a barbecue out here on the patio?"

Taylor muttered something on the way out. Apparently he wasn't fond of barbecues, but we were thrilled.

Mrs. Benson announced, "You haven't lived until you've had my husband's famous barbecued chicken."

"Made all the better by my wife's very own, secret recipe barbecue sauce," added Mr. Benson, with a nod for us and a wink for his wife.

Jack said his deli makes the best potato salad, and he would be happy to bring some. Gus and I agreed to go to town with him, but first Mrs. Benson asked me to try calling Aunt Jennifer again.

She answered after the first ring and was delighted to hear I was okay. She said my parents had called looking for me and she had been worried ever since. When she asked if my parents knew I was safe, I said Mrs. Benson wanted to talk to her.

I handed the phone to Mrs. Benson who explained who she was and how we met. She told her she wanted to talk privately about an issue involving me and my parents. Mrs. Benson invited Aunt Jennifer to the barbecue and said they could talk later in the evening.

I needed to sit down. My head dropped to my chest as I slumped onto the window seat. Now it's really out, I thought.

Mrs. Benson hung up the phone and sat down next to me. "She's on her way," she said softly.

I looked at her, not knowing what to say.

"Don't worry," she said. "It takes a lot of courage to tell. You did the right thing. Now that we know, we can help you."

Mrs. Benson smiled and stood up. "So, how about that potato salad?"

Chapter 9

Face to Face

During the drive to town, I sat quietly watching the scenery go by while Jack and Gus talked. Jack has been living on his own for almost a year and his job keeps him pretty busy. Although they talked about things they used to do together, I could hear a touch of sadness in Gus's voice. It was obvious he missed having his brother around. You could feel the love between them. I thought how lucky they were to have each other.

As we pulled up to the deli, I noticed some familiar faces in a van across the street.

"Look! It's them!"

"Who, what?" said Jack looking in the direction I was pointing.

"Getting out of the van. It's Holly and Mace," I screamed in a whisper.

"Do you see Cody?" asked Gus, leaning forward to get a better look.

"Get down!" I insisted. "They're coming this way."

Gus and I ducked down on the seat until Jack said it was clear. They had gone into the deli.

Jack talked quickly, trying to sound calm. "Okay, I'll keep them inside as long as I can. You two go next door and call the police, and then stay there!"

After Jack left, Gus turned to me while reaching for the door handle. "You call the police. I'm gonna see if Cody is in the van."

"But Gus…" I started. It was too late. He shot off running, limping slightly from his twisted ankle.

In the jewelry store, I quickly explained about Mace and Holly and asked the salesman to call the police. "Ask for Detective Sheaffer," I said. "He'll know what to do."

I went outside to find Gus. He was nowhere in sight. Then I remembered that Holly and Mace didn't know about me. Gus was the one in danger.

I had to move quickly. I needed to know exactly where they were and how long it could take before they returned to the van.

I tried to act casual as I walked passed the deli window, while my heart did jumping jacks in my chest. Inside, Holly and Mace were fidgeting impatiently at the counter while Jack worked very slowly on their order, whistling the whole time.

I had to stall them even more until the police could arrive. I ran to Jack's car, ripped open my bag, and grabbed the lotion and the powder. Noticing a ballpoint pen shaped like a race car on the dashboard, I grabbed that, too.

I glanced toward the deli—no one coming yet—then ran across the street to their van. The front tire on the passenger side, facing away from the street, was my first stop. I pushed the pen into the valve stem and held it in place. I quietly called out to Gus but there was no response, only the steady hissing of air leaving the tire.

I moved around to where I could see into the deli. There were more people inside. It was hard to tell what was going on.

Again, I went back behind the far side of the van. Now I had the lotion. I squeezed the tube with both hands, allowing the lotion to ooze out and spread all over the door handle on the passenger's side. That should slow one of them down a bit. I moved to the back of the van and soon heard voices coming closer. Holly and Mace were complaining about the service in the deli.

An explosion of noise and activity soon followed them: sirens in the distance, screeching tires around the corner, the van door opening, a dog barking.

I ran around to the front of the van, passing Holly as she walked toward the passenger side.

"Hey, what the…" she shouted, noticing the flat tire as her hand slipped on the messy door handle.

Mace was leaning into the van, yelling something as the screaming sirens arrived.

Armed with my next weapon I moved in close to Mace, tapped him on the back and, with all the courage I could gather, I yelled, "Hey, slime brain!" Well that definitely got his attention!

Surprised and angry, he whipped around so fast I had to struggle to keep from falling, but not before I hit him with a healthy dose of Tropical Garden scented powder. It went everywhere—in his eyes, in his nose, in his mouth. All he could do was cough and sneeze as he blindly tried to grab the cause of his misery—ME!

As I regained my balance and turned to get help, I ran right into one of the policemen.

"Got her," he shouted with a tight grip on my arms.

"Freeze!" commanded the policewoman at Mace as another officer approached him from behind. Holly, already handcuffed, was being led to one of the patrol cars.

Jack ran across the street from the deli, calling out to the policeman to let me go. Gus climbed into the front seat of the van, holding tight to Cody who was squirming to get down. Meanwhile, all the commotion was attracting a small crowd.

"Gus, are you all right?" Jack asked.

"Yeah," said Gus. "There must have been ten knots in this rope. I didn't think I'd ever get Cody untied, and there was so much noise out here—"

He stopped in mid-sentence as he looked up and at the scene around the van. There were police cars, flashing lights, and officers everywhere; not to mention a rather nice smelling powder on the ground and on Mace who was being questioned.

Jack saw the powder tin in my hand and with a big grin said, "Nice job! Where'd you get—"

"Wow!" interrupted Gus. "What happened here? I heard the sirens. I just figured everyone was at the deli. Hey, what's that white stuff, tear gas?"

Gus had such an innocent look on his face, Jack and I had to laugh.

Jack nodded at me and said, "You tell him about the powder."

"Maybe I should tell him about the lotion," then added, "Oh, and the tire."

They both stared at me and in one surprised voice asked, "What tire?!"

Dinner that night at the Bensons was great! Everyone talked of the daring rescue. Even a couple of the police officers came to thank us again.

Detective Sheaffer stopped by to tell us that most of the Benson's jewelry had been recovered, but would be needed as evidence. He also told us that Mace already had a police record for stealing and, with these new charges, would probably go to jail. Holly was too young to go to jail, but they were working to get her into a program to help kids in trouble.

Gus would stay with Jack until their parents returned from their trip the next day. Jack said he would help Gus explain.

Aunt Jennifer was there; she and Mrs. Benson had a long private talk. When they finished, they both hugged me and assured me everything would be fine.

Later that evening, a policewoman talked with me about my parents and took notes. She also told me about a local group that helps children and their families when there are reports of abuse. She then told me I might not be able to go back home for a while—not until my mom and dad were well enough for me to return.

Aunt Jennifer explained gently, "Your parents need time for this, and right now it's not a safe place for you to be. I would like you to come and stay with me, Chris, if you want to."

She looked into my eyes, waiting for a response.

How I wish this wasn't happening! I didn't want to leave home, not really. I wished my parents would just *be* better once they knew how much they were hurting me.

I took a deep breath and let out an even longer sigh, exhausted from trying to figure it all out.

I was glad Aunt Jennifer wanted me to stay with her.

I hugged her then, feeling both sad and relieved. "Thank you," I whispered in her ear. She gave me a little squeeze and held me even more.

Chapter 10

New Beginnings

Living with Aunt Jennifer and Uncle Martin was different from living at home. I liked it at their house but I also missed my parents and my room.

Anne, my counselor, helped me understand that, by telling about the abuse, my parents could get the help they needed. But, she said, they also had to want to get better by learning to work through their problems

instead of taking them out on me. I hoped
they would.

Besides having to move, I guess the big-
gest change was not being so afraid anymore. I still had trouble falling asleep at
night, but Anne said that wasn't unusual. It
could take a while to feel safe again. She also
said it takes time to get used to the sounds
and smells and feel of a new place, even
when you like it. I also knew how much my
aunt and uncle loved me and was sure they
would protect me.

Eventually I told them everything. Aunt
Jennifer said she wished I could have told
her sooner, but she understood how afraid I
must have been.

One Sunday, about a month after I
moved in, I was sitting on the porch swing
with Jasmine the cat and thinking about
Gus. I had tried to call him, but could never reach him. I still wore the ring he gave

me. I hoped he was all right. I hoped my parents would be all right. I hoped I did the right thing.

Jasmine jumped off the swing, licked her striped paws, and walked lazily across the yard. The caw-caw of a crow in a nearby tree warned of the cat's approach. Jasmine hunkered down flat against the grass as she spied something that only cat eyes can see. In a flash, she bolted into the bushes, then up and over the fence—off on another adventure.

I stretched out in her place and snuggled my head into one of the pillows. Drifting in and out of a very relaxed and sleepy space, I soon heard a clear and familiar voice.

"Remember the rings of water moving out."

Her words had that same enchanting effect as that night in the woods. I almost

121

held my breath as if somehow that would prevent her, and the moment, from fading away. It was the lady of light. I couldn't see her like before, but I knew it was her.

Then, almost as if I were watching a movie, I saw myself sitting by the river under the oak tree, tossing stones into the water. I watched how each stone made little waves that moved out in a circle from the center. Soon the waves settled and became part of the river again.

I shifted slightly to a more comfortable position on the swing, trying to keep the picture of the river in my mind.

Again, she spoke. "It hasn't always been easy for you, but still, your love and kindness has come through.

"Always believe in yourself, Chris. There are many, many places in life. Know that each one is important. Be yourself, and your place will be the best that it can be. Trust what has happened. Trust me, Chris."

Then I heard my own voice. "But who are you?"

"I am the voice inside you that told you there was something wrong and to ask for help. I am the voice that said you would not always be afraid, but you were too afraid to listen. Now you have listened and you have learned. Love me. Love yourself. I am you, Chris."

My mind went blank. I must have been in shock. I heard another voice.

"Chris, Chris, come on! Wake up! What are you doing, checking your eyelids for light leaks?"

I opened my eyes and they quickly filled with happy tears. There stood Gus, holding Cody.

"Hey, I didn't realize I had such an effect on people," he said with that sly grin of his.

"I am just so happy to see you. I tried to call. How have you been?"

"Great, just great, but I've been real busy. Mr. and Mrs. Benson gave Cody to me! Their son found him somewhere and could never find the owner. He's too busy at school, and the Bensons aren't home much, so they gave him to me. Isn't that great?! And anyway, I guess Taylor's allergic to him."

I smiled, remembering their butler.

Gus continued, "I finally talked to my mom and dad. They were pretty shook up when they heard everything. But we talked it all out and decided to spend more time together. One day a week will be family day. Even Jack liked the idea and would come when he could. He and I are going camping this weekend."

It was good to see Gus again. He seemed lighter somehow, even for him, but more relaxed than when we were in the woods, like he didn't have to pretend to be someone he wasn't. He could be himself. How could he be anyone else?

Cody had been squirming with excitement the whole time. Gus put him on the seat cushion and he immediately sprang into my lap and started licking my face. I petted and hugged him until he settled in next to me.

"You know," Gus said, his voice turning serious, "I never could talk to anyone like I can talk to you, Chris. You listen and you care. If it wasn't for you, I don't think I ever would have said anything." He went on playfully, "Who knows where I'd be right now—maybe hitchin' my way across country, hoppin' freight trains, going from job to job…"

I responded to his drama with a smile. He tossed one back a little sheepishly and stuffed his hands into his pockets. I was lucky to have met Gus, and I knew we would always be very special friends—just like we promised.

Gus said, "I brought you something."

He handed me a small box tied with string. As I removed the string and lifted the lid, he said, "I know you like flowers. I mean you were always looking at them. Besides, that old chain ring ain't nothin' special and, well, you are, so I wanted you to have something no one else has. Jack helped me make it. Jewelry is his hobby. Anyway, I hope you like it."

When I pulled back the tissue paper, my breath caught in my throat. To my total surprise, lying on a cloud of cotton was a bracelet more beautiful than I could ever have imagined. I couldn't speak. I couldn't even breathe because in the center of the silver band, almost separate from the rest as if suspended, was a flower, it was blue... and it was a rose.

A playful breeze swirled around me before continuing on its way across Lakeview Park. Staring off into space, I must have looked like I was in some kind of trance as I remembered that time so long ago.

Glancing down, three spellbound children were silent. Theresa was the first to speak.

"When was all this?" she asked.

"Just before your mom and dad were married—about twelve years ago."

"That means Aunt Jennifer ..." started Theresa.

"Is your mother," I said, finishing her thought for her.

"What about your parents?" asked Roger.

"They weren't ready to work through their problems. They did try for a while, though. They even went to a group that would teach them how to be better parents. But they didn't stay with it long enough for real change to take place. I never did go back. Sad, isn't it?"

Theresa nodded. "What about Gus and Cody?"

"Gus and his family worked everything out. With some help they learned how to talk about their feelings and how important it is to listen to each other. Gus is now in college studying to be a veterinarian." I paused and added thoughtfully, "We're still real good friends."

"And Cody?" asked Theresa again.

"Oh, he's still around. He lives with Gus's family while Gus is in school."

We were all quiet for a moment. Sara carefully broke the silence. "Are you glad you told?"

"Oh, yes," I said. "I realize even more now what a frightening time that was for me. I tried so hard to be good—to do all the right things and do well in school—so they wouldn't hurt me. But I know now that my grades and my behavior had nothing to do with it."

"So it wasn't your fault? You didn't make them mad?" asked Sara. Before I could answer, she added softly, "Do you think they loved you?"

I sighed at such big questions, the same ones I had asked myself. "No, it wasn't my fault. Even if they were mad at me that wasn't why I was abused. You may get angry over something someone does or says but that doesn't give you the right to hurt them. And I don't think my father thought much about whether he was hurting me or not.

"As far as loving me…" I paused wanting to choose the best words. "I believe they have love in their hearts. I believe everyone does. But sometimes things happen to make people want to hide what they feel. They may have loved me but didn't know how to show it. But that doesn't mean I wasn't lovable—just as you are lovable and worthwhile now.

Sara lowered her head.

"Why do you think it happened?" asked Theresa.

"I don't know for sure. I think he was mistreated when he was young and didn't have anyone to talk to about it or protect him from it. I don't think he's ever faced how that made him feel. And he still carries that pain around inside.

"Sometimes when people are treated like this, especially from people they care about, they become afraid to talk about it as if bringing it up will make it hurt all over again. They may also think that no one will believe them, or no one will care, or that somehow it was their fault. They pretend it doesn't matter, but it does matter. Not ever talking about something that hurts only makes it hurt more. I think they are still afraid, so they don't say anthing and hope it will all go away.

"But that doesn't excuse them. Child abuse is never okay. Adults are supposed to protect children from being hurt even if no one protected them. The only chance I had of making it stop was to find someone to tell."

"Or you could run away," offered Roger.

"That's true," I said. "But, you know, I didn't think of it as running away at the time. I was just so scared. I had to do something. So I left, hoping I could figure out what to do. I didn't think much further ahead than that. And running away isn't always the best answer, although you might feel you have no other choice. You still need to tell someone sometime."

"What if you tell someone and they don't believe you or they don't do anything?" asked Sara.

"Then you find someone else to tell. A secret that hurts might be a secret that needs to be told. If you, or someone you know is being hurt, find someone to tell, someone you can trust. Give them a chance to be the caring people that they are."

"Like my mom," said Theresa.

"And Gus," said Roger.

"And many others," I added, lazily stretching my arms over my head.

"Can I see your bracelet?" asked Roger.

"Me, too?" asked Theresa moving in a little closer.

"Sure," I said and released the catch on the chain that had been added a few years ago.

I leaned back against the tree as the children examined my bracelet.

"Wow," Roger said as he pulled out a magnifying glass. "Gus made this?"

I thought of Gus and how our friendship had grown from a chance meeting in the woods. Or was there something more, some kind of destiny? Did we meet for a reason? Anyway, it was a turning point for both of us. He helped me see that, although awful things were happening to me, the world wasn't an awful place. And we both learned to speak up about our feelings and our ideas.

Through eyes made misty by a flood of memories and mixed emotions, I looked at the children before me and smiled. They, too, are so much more than they realize.

Roger handed me the bracelet and began packing up his jars. Theresa had gathered up our trash and joined Roger in carrying the first load to the car. Sara sat quietly, staring at a bunch of dandelions she had picked from around our blanket.

I wasn't sure how to say this but I started anyway. "If you ever need someone to talk to…"

Sara lifted her head and held the bright yellow flowers out to me. I could see the tears in her eyes. It was a small gesture, but one that overflowed with meaning for both of us. A tear escaped and rolled down my cheek as I accepted her gift.

Sara came to me then, wrapping her arms around my neck. She nestled her head on my shoulder and held me in a hug so precious. She understood. My story, a part of my life, had touched her deeply. Maybe by sharing my story, I have made a positive difference in her life.

I looked at the blue rose of my bracelet and thought about how far I've come. There is so much I want to do, and so many ways I can help.

I thought of the rings of water and knew I was sharing the knowledge. I thought, too, of the lady of light and knew she would always be with me.

Filled with a sense of purpose, I smiled as I held Sara and the flowers and realized what a truly lucky person I am.

More from the Author

I thought you might have questions about the story or the topic, so be sure to check out these last few pages!

And remember, although bad things may happen, the good news is that there are people in this world, and in your community, who will help. The hard part is asking. As victims, we are afraid of causing harm to someone else, even the person hurting us. We just want it to stop.

Regardless of your age, if you are being hurt in any way, find someone to talk to. It may not be easy at first, but it is a lot easier than continuing to be hurt by it. I promise you it will get better, if you get the help you need and deserve.

You are not alone. It is not your fault.
You truly are a lovable and
worthwhile person!

About the Title

During the early stages of writing this book, an image of a blue rose appeared very clearly to me one day while I sat in meditation. I had never seen a *blue* rose, which led me to think they must be very special. I have since learned that blue colored roses do not exist in nature, as far as we know.

Since ancient times, the idea of a blue rose has held a sense of magic and mystery. So, perhaps by fate, it found its place in this story. Whether we find one in a garden or in our imagination, a blue rose can remind us that we, too, are unique and anything is possible.

About the Illustrations

All of the illustrations in this book are drawn by hand. I used colored pencils, except for the drawing in the chapter entitled, *Lady of Light*. To create a softer and more enchanting effect, I used pastels for the area behind the trees.

I don't have official training in the arts but I love to draw. As you can see, I am all about the details. I enjoy creating images that have a life-like quality while holding a sense of magic. I mention this to encourage you to find a way, that is special to you, to express your imagination.

People & Places

This story is a work of fiction, but it is based on my experience as a victim of child abuse and the lessons I've learned since. Some of the locations and characters were inspired by places I have seen and people I have known.

- For a while, I lived in a house on the edge of the woods just as I have described.

- Lakeview Park, with all of its sights and activities, existed under another name: Metropolitan Park.

- The *grandmother tree* is in Hawaii, where I lived for 14 years. Instead of a river, she stood along a path with a view of mountains and waterfalls.

- The dream of flying is one I often had as a child.

- The *lady of light* represents a number of experiences and lessons.

- Gus is based, mostly, on a boy I knew for a short time in high school. He gave me the chain ring mentioned in the book—a simple act of kindness that always brings a smile.

- As an adult, I had a Yorkshire Terrier named Kelsey. She was a bundle of love for all of her 14 years.

- The message of Hawk is a reference to Native American spirituality. My study of it helped enormously in my healing and continues to guide me today.

- The original draft of this book was written with a Sheaffer fountain pen. That is how Detective Sheaffer got his name.

- Anne, Chris's counselor, was the name of my counselor in Hawaii. She was an amazing woman who helped many survivors. She reviewed the original draft of this book.

Phone Numbers & Websites

The organizations on this page have counselors available *all day, every day.* Call if you have questions, need help right away, or want to find someone to talk to in your area. Their websites also have information you might find useful.

YourlifeYourvoice.org   1-800-448-3000
This *website* is for kids, teens, and young adults to share concerns in positive and creative ways. Counselors are available for your questions through the *hotline,* online chat, text, or email. Call or check the website for details. It is a service of BoysTown.org.

ChildHelp.org   1-800-422-4453
National Child Abuse Hotline

TheHotline.org   1-800-799-7233
National Domestic Violence Hotline

It helps to know that:

- Calls *may* be answered by a recording, so you might have to wait a few minutes to connect with a person. Don't give up!

- If you are not getting the help you are looking for, try another hotline or organization.

- To find more resources, or if the ones listed have changed, try an Internet search for *hotlines*, *helplines*, or the topic you are interested in.

- Your school or library may also have helpful books and resources.

Remember, if you or someone you know is ever in danger and need help right away from fire, police, or medical services, call:

9-1-1

Get the help you deserve.
Many people care enough to help.

A Message For Adults

Believe the child. It is far more likely that their disclosures of abuse are true. If you question their truth, imagine what might prompt such a claim. Children are afraid to tell. They fear:

* They won't be believed
* What will happen to them for telling
* What will happen to the offender
* What will happen to their world

When a child has decided to trust you with their secret, earn their trust by enlisting help. If you cannot offer the emotional support necessary, refer them to someone who can in a way that lets them know it was okay to tell you.

Refer to *Phone Numbers & Websites*, *About Reporting*, and *Adult Survivors*.

Reading This Book To Children

- Let them interrupt with questions or comments as they are ready.
- Allow and acknowledge their feelings, whatever they may be.
- Let them explore what the characters may be feeling.
- Demonstrate by your actions and words that there are adults who can be trusted to listen, to care, to help.

About Reporting

Most adults want to help but don't know what to do. Learn more about this and other topics here: helpguide.org

Call your local child welfare/protection agency and ask what happens when a report is made. Find contact numbers for your area here: childwelfare.gov

ADULT SURVIVORS

There are many organizations and private individuals working to prevent violence, encourage survivors, and brighten our world. When you are ready, seek them out, join with them, or create a new way of sharing your light.

Adult Survivors of Child Abuse is an international self-help support group. Visit their website for free access to their *Survivor to Thriver Manual*.

ascasupport.org

2-1-1 is a free confidential information referral and helpline. Call 2-1-1 or visit their website to find a 2-1-1 that serves your area.

211.org

Try an online search: *support for survivors of abuse* and check for resources on those sites to find one that's right for you.

Also by Debbie Jenae

Be An Inspiration!

101 Things You Can Do To Prevent Child Abuse
A resource for adults to promote positive action,
advocacy, and healing.

Visit DebbieJenae.com

Acknowledgments

This story was written more than 25 years ago. At that time, few publishers invested in books about child abuse, no matter how encouraging. For various reasons, *The Blue Rose*, as it was called then, went on the shelf for a while but stayed close to my heart. It's been quite a journey bringing it to you.

In that effort, I am ever so grateful to Sue Bott for her grammar and editing expertise, Anne-Sophie Hug for her insight and support, and Kevin Belstler whose heartfelt response was priceless.

Very special thanks to my daughter Ashley who was the first to read the first version of this, my first book. Mahalo!

And to Anne Selten, who urged me to seek publication. Her wisdom and compassion brought light through dark times. Her spirit is with me still.

About the Author

Debbie Jenae has lived in six states across the U.S. including Hawaii where, for seven years, she was a voice for abused and neglected children in court. Her dedication earned

Photo by Kevin

her an award nomination for outstanding volunteer service by the Hawaii governor's office.

Debbie is a survivor with a passion for empowering others. A certified master handwriting analyst, her presentations and more than 300 published articles encourage understanding of behavior and potential. She is the author of *Be An Inspiration!* and founder of Inspired 101, a resource for positive action, advocacy, and healing. She lives in California.